Betsy and Michelle

Betsy AND Michelle

THE ADVENTURES OF *Betsy* AND *Michelle*

MANJULA BAJAJ

HARRY BAJAJ

First Published 2015

ISBN 13: 978-81-7386-312-7
ISBN 10: 81-7386-312-1

Published by
BOOKS FOR ALL
A-6, 2nd Floor, Nimri Commercial Centre,
Ashok Vihar Phase 4, Delhi - 110 052 (India)
Tel.: +91 - 11 - 2730 2453
Fax.: +91 - 11 - 4706 1936
website: www.LPPindia.com
e-mail: info@LPPindia.com

PRINTED IN INDIA

Betsy AND Michelle

Betsy was a Golden Retriever, a big furry dog, with a bigger heart. Michelle or Mishu, as she is called at times, is a Pug. A tiny dog, if you compare her with Betsy in terms of size. She is smaller than the average Pug. If Betsy had sat upon Michelle that would have been the end of Michelle, just as it would have also been curtains for little Michelle if Betsy had bitten her or mauled her. She generously accepted Michelle as another member of the family, and I think she was amused at the size of Michelle. Betsy was unique as is Michelle and both have their own idiosyncrasies. Both conquered our hearts. Though Betsy is no more, memories of her and Michelle live. Their pranks, clean and simple, evoked so much joy and affection. I would like to share some of those days with you I always felt that our family was complete with husband Harry, son Rahul and daughter Aditi. I did not know how wrong I was. The best was yet to come and in 1998 and we added Betsy to our family. She was a gorgeous female pup, with soft brown eyes, honey coloured fur, and a great tendency to get into mischief. She grew into a beautiful, furry Golden Retriever, with a perpetually drooling tongue, a tail that was on auto pilot since it wagged all the time and a terrifyingly loud bark. We named her Betsy because we felt that in some mysterious way she had to be named Betsy! At times I am at times not too sure if she was an addition to our family or if she adopted us, but the story goes back several years to the South Indian city of Bengaluru or Bangalore, as it was called then.

My husband's colleague Sanjeev was working in Manipal and sought my advice regarding a dog his family wanted. Since I had a dog before my marriage in Bangalore, I was regarded as an expert on canines. Sanjeev wanted a dog that would be part of the family and who would tolerate toddlers and children around him. I unhesitatingly gave him my opinion. I said, a Golden Retriever any day. The next thing was Sanjeev was pleading with me to help him procure one. I found myself saying that I would help him.

So, on a Sunday morning I flipped through the newspapers, scrolling through the ads for pets. I got lucky; there was an advertisement which said golden retriever pups were for sale at a place that was not too far from home. I promptly called the number and asked if they had male pups for sale and the reply was, 'Yes, we do have male pups available and they are at the right age for separation from their mum!' I went to see them and was greeted by seven adorable, healthy looking pups.

I stood, for the next 15 minutes stood watching them play, and I wondered which one to pick; then one of the pups came bouncing over. He wagged his tail as if he'd found a long lost friend. He clambered over my shoes and rubbed himself on my legs. 'I'll take him,' I said. He was named Pluto. The name was apt for him and he grew up to be a robust, handsome dog. Sanjeev was delighted and took him to his home in Chandigarh. I thought that was the end of that and put Sanjeev and Pluto out of my mind. Scarcely three months had passed when Sanjeev called with another request. The problem was that the whole family loved Pluto, including his mother in law! Now he had to procure a female golden retriever for her! I could sense a bit of a dilemma for Sanjeev and I said I would try. I called the same number and this time sure enough they did have a female pup available. Yes, she was a Golden Retriever. Yes, they would be happy to hold her for me till I got there. And when I saw her she was another beauty; I named her Lara and brought her home. Sanjeev flew in from Chandigarh to pick her up.

Lara

Lara and Pluto took to one another like tea and milk. Sanjeev's mother in law was delighted. He was immensely grateful and he asked me how could he repay me for my trouble? We were travelling overseas at that time and I was preoccupied with the ten thousand things one has to do when relocating. But Sanjeev persisted and finally I told him that we would like a pup from Lara and Pluto, whenever we returned. We left and I put Sanjeev, Pluto and Lara from my mind. I had enough on my plate bringing up my own two little ones - Rahul and Aditi in a foreign country. We were going to be abroad close to 5 years.

Betsy

Zooming back to 1998, we returned to India, to New Delhi. Sanjeev had stayed in touch with us and called on us when we had settled down. As he was leaving he casually dropped his bombshell. Lara was pregnant and the vet has said she would deliver any time next week. Were we still interested in that pup? In our family a kind of a democracy rules and when the family learnt that a pup would be a new addition, bedlam broke out. Did the family want a pup? What a question! 'Now who is going to look after that pup?' I asked. I wanted the children to assume responsibility for their actions; 'We all are', they chorused! A roster of duties was already in the back of my mind. I had a word with my husband, Harry. He just grunted and carried on with his work. That grunt could be a yes, it could be a no, or it could be a kind of 'not-now-lets-see-how-it-goes' response. It all depends on its interpretation and mine was a solid 'yes'. Sanjeev delivered the pup and that's how Betsy entered our family. She was born on 10th August 1998. She was beautiful. Simply that. Other words to describe her are embellishments. She entered our lives, and took them over. Some of the events that I am going to describe would never happen in Europe, but here in India they may not even cause a raised eyebrow.

Weaning off

She was soon weaned off her puppy habits of chewing anything and everything that she came across - be it shoes, the legs of the bed or the other bits of furniture that occupied the room. She had a notion that these were placed there for her to sample. She particularly relished socks and she would not rest till she had them in tatters. We quickly learn to keep these out of her reach. I gave her an occasional bone to chew; she played with it more than she chewed it. As she grew she became increasingly gorgeous; I spent time grooming her and slowly taught her simple commands. She was a quick learner and her vocabulary had increased. She was remarkably obedient. She had loads of patience; it's amazing that when she was served her meal and she would patiently wait for a 'Go and eat' command. She would look at it and droll but she would not touch or even smell it, till ordered to eat. With that she would tear into her food. She learnt, 'Go for walk', and would launch into a frenzied search for her leash. Having located it, she would grab it and triumphantly bring it and place it at my feet, all the time wagging her tail, as if to say, 'Come on, come on, let's go, what is the delay all about?' She loved playing with a ball, and if thrown would run after it and fetch it. She was soon house trained and not once did she dirty the house after that.

Betsy

TURNS

ONE

By the time Betsy was a year old, she relished her meals and her walks. These were the two focal points in her life. Breakfast was the major meal of the day. This was had with the rest of the family in the dining room. She preferred home cooked meals to commercial products for dogs. She had a bowl in which her breakfast was served - an egg, a bowl of porridge, and occasionally rotis, or bread. She was a typical Indian dog and ate Punjabi food with gusto. Allu paranthas (roti stuffed with boiled and mashed potatoes, without the usual spices) were a particular favourite, but could be happily discarded for a juicy bone with meat on it. She had a weakness for bananas and I wondered at times if she ever had a monkey as an ancestor somewhere. She loved apples but bananas were the preferred flavour any time.

When it was time for a walk I just had to say, 'Betsy, go for walk?' and the result was a cacophony of sound and confusion. She would run and get her leash and wait for it to be placed around her neck. If there was a delay, she would protest with a vigorous bark, which could be heard several houses away. It was incumbent that whoever took her for her walk had to place her leash at a designated site. At times, this standard operating procedure broke down, and the leash having been misplaced, Betsy when told to find her leash would not rest till it had been located. She would appear triumphantly, holding the leash firmly clenched between her jaws. It was implied that having located the missing leash a walk was an undeniable reward. Betsy loved the car and always was ready for a joy ride. She had to sit by the window, and the glass had to be rolled down. She would stick her head out and simply enjoy the rush of air as we cruised sedately along the road. Harry usually drove and he was a careful driver, fully aware that an excitable dog was our passenger in the rear seat.

I had to sit next to her, holding on to her collar. If Betsy saw another dog she would bark and if she became excited I would simply shut the window. Peace would prevail after that. She did not hesitate to bark at any creature she encountered, be it a cow or buffalo roaming the street, or another canine or anybody she did not like.

Betsy SMELLS A RAT!

Vasant Kunj is a popular locality in south west Delhi with neat rows of identical government constructed flats. It has a number of blocks, with each block having its own market so everything that one needed was within easy reach. People who live here are affluent, with the occupants of each flat owning at least two cars. Like all up market areas in any major metropolis, people here mind their own business by and large. But more on that later.

The problem in Vasant Kunj, at least when we were there, were the rats. The rat is a survivor; it is omnivorous, and can live on any food. It is not what you would call, fastidious. It has been around a long time and reportedly the Romans brought it into Britain. I was not too concerned about the Romans bring the rat along with them as they trotted into Britain, but I was not wildly enthusiastic about rats in my home. We had noticed rat droppings on the floor and on a couple of occasions I had found that food that had been inadvertently left outside had been nibbled. When I pointed this out to my son Rahul, he helpfully pointed out that I was using the wrong word as the correct word was 'gnawed' and not nibbled. Boys!

When I brought it up with Harry who is a busy doctor, the response was, 'How interesting. Did you know dear, that the rat is also called 'Rattus rattus' and it wiped out approximately 200 million people in a pandemic called the Black Death around 1350 in Europe?' Husbands! I could have throttled them both, but I took a deep breath instead and went off to make a cup of tea while I pondered over my problem. I noticed that Betsy was in the kitchen, a territory that had been declared as out of bound for her. She had been given to understand that as far as the kitchen was concerned, she was persona non grata. I took another deep breath and was ready to explode when I noted that Betsy had her nose to the ground, was moving excitedly and wagging her tail furiously. I stood and watched amused as she gave an excited yelp. It became obvious that she had smelt something on the ground. I had important chores to finish so I shooed her away.

A couple of days later I was in the drawing room with Harry. We were immersed in our plans for the future, when there were a series of sharp, short barks and clearly the source was Betsy and by the sound of it she had breached protocol and was making merry in my kitchen. Both Harry and I went to the kitchen. There was Betsy. Her eyes were gleaming with joy and she was wagging her tail 180 degrees and making happy grunting sounds with her mouth closed. At first I couldn't figure out what Betsy was up to till I suddenly heard the squeal of the rat in her jaws and saw the tail of that wretched creature fluttering desperately on one side. Betsy was clearly enjoying herself. She had somehow caught that unfortunate animal and the only part that was visible was its tail which was waving from the side of her mouth. Flabbergasted, I frantically tried everything to get her to drop the rat, even went to the extent of cajoling her with a bone. It made matters worse; she held her jaw tighter and obstinately refused to open her mouth. Clearly she and I had very different ideas about this. She was enjoying herself. Hugely. I was petrified that she would pick up some horrible canine equivalent of the Black Death. Normally Betsy treats Harry like some of his patients - like god. But no way was Betsy going to let that rat go, and even Harry's command was ignored. When she realized that we were not going to relent on this one, she, in a flash and a large gulp, swallowed the rat, tail and all. She then came up and it was clear in her doggie brain that she had won the doggie equivalent of the world cup in cricket. She preened in front and expected a pat and a few words of praise. I was quite stunned and I rushed to the telephone to call her vet and take his sage counsel. When I narrated the incident the Doctor laughed and assured me that Betsy would be fine because Goldens are carnivorous. That was reassuring. Clearly Betsy was all right and remained so. We narrated the incident to the kids in the evening. Aditi has always been concerned about hygiene and she felt that the least we could do was to brush her teeth. Unknown to me the two procured a tooth-brush, (soft bristles, mind you), and tried to get her to show her teeth and stay still for long enough for them to brush her teeth. No sir, there was no way that Betsy would stay still enough for them to do that. She shook them off and stalked away, the kids followed, determined to improve her oral hygiene. They persisted and that's when I heard her snarl, but that was it. She refused to attack them, whatever the provocation. A snarl. A warning. It was enough. The kids left her alone, all thoughts of oral hygiene forgotten.

Instead of keeping a cat we decided to train Betsy. She sure beat all cats; when she was told Betsy "Chooha" (rat), she was up an about ready to hunt the rat and wouldn't rest till she caught it. That approach worked and the rat population in a mysterious rodent way realized that they would become extinct if they ever wandered into our house. Betsy was lethal.

She enjoyed playing with them as well, but she had to kill them in the end; having caught one she would settle down in a quiet corner. She would release the poor blighter and as it scurried away, out would come a paw and settle on its tail. She looked at it struggling and would hit it with her other paw and stun it. Having knocked it out, she would wait for it to revive and then the game would begin again. When she realized we did not approve of these sporting activities, she stopped displaying the captured rats as trophies to us and simply played her games with them and when she had enough she simply executed them.

THE GARBAGE COLLECTOR

There is something in dogs about garbage collectors. All dogs have an undying hatred of garbage collectors. In the doggie kingdom, garbage collectors were designed for their sadistic satisfaction. They are made to be barked at, snarled at and if the doggie equivalent of Nirvana holds good, perhaps even a bite could be had of that unfortunate's ankles as he runs from that furious canine. Now that would be simply rapturous! Betsy felt that the garbage collector was definitely a malignant species, created solely for her to bite. And if that poor chap took to his heels when he came in a face to face confrontation with Betsy, she would be absolutely delighted to chase him! Perhaps as she snapped at his ankles that poor chap could run even faster! In her doggie brain this was definitely a moment to be savoured as she chased away another garbage collector!

As a puppy Betsy harboured no ill feelings against garbage collectors. But as she crossed six months chronologically, she developed an undying hatred for that species. Perhaps it was something to do with his technique or the way he would proclaim his arrival by ringing the door bell. Now we lived in a rented flat and we never had a say in the selection of that device. All of that was done by the builder. The bell that had been installed rang with vehemence, urgency and noise, all mixed in equal measure and with such intensity that would have a person with terminal somnolence doing calisthenics in no time at all. All he had to do was to listen to that blasted thing ring. Its effect on the sleeping Betsy was to have her leaping a foot high, instantly alert, fur standing up, tongue out, barking and snarling with great gusto. The barking was a full volume sound that arose deep in her chest, gathered momentum as it rumbled past her throat, and was expelled in an explosive, ear drum shattering sound. A canine equivalent of 'going for broke'. So noisy was her bark that all the folks in those closely clustered houses in that block knew that the garbage collector had come. That worthy too derived a perverse thrill in getting Betsy all worked up. The entrance was locked always. Betsy could bark at the garbage man from indoors, while he was free to taunt her from the exterior. He would never do it while any of the family was around, but the moment he realized that no one was around and that Betsy could not accost him; he had no hesitation in teasing her. Thus resulted another episode of furious and angry barking. I caught him teasing her one day; I explained to him that it was not a nice thing to do, but it had no effect. The only change was that he would never tease her if any member of the family was around.

The drill that was followed in every flat was the same. The garbage collector would ring the bell, and in all likelihood wake up the occupants as he would collect the garbage at 5 am, when most occupants were still asleep. It never bothered me because I had to be up early anyway to make breakfast, make the lunch, pack it for Harry, and for both the kids to take to their school; Betsy too had to be taken out to allow her to do her business; so all in all the ringing of the bell at 5am was no major deal. Except on a Sunday, when I liked to laze for a while, and expected Harry to make the morning cup of tea. This would be followed by a leisurely browse through the newspapers and a leisurely breakfast. Anyway, when the garbage man had rung his bell, any person in the family would take the garbage and hand it in person to the garbage collector, who would cart it away in his smelly, hand pushed cart. If the door was not opened in the space of 15 to 30 seconds there would be another short and impatient ring and if that worthy did not get any response from the inhabitants of the house he would move on and the garbage stayed uncollected. Why not place the garbage in a bin with a lid and leave it outside, for the garbage collector to collect? This was a bad idea as I had found out the hard way. There were a few strays in the locality (well it was their locality too) who had learnt presumably by trial and error that if a garbage bin could be knocked over there was a likelihood of its contents being available as the lid disassociated itself from the bin. The plastic bag in which the garbage was stored was easily ripped apart by their sharp teeth and claws. After I had cleaned up the mess of haphazardly strewn waste a couple of times, I learnt that it was easier to hand over the garbage to the johnnie who collected it. Even if it meant answering the door at 5 am.

It was a cold Sunday morning. Harry and I were lazing in bed, Aditi was still asleep, Rahul had taken Betsy for her morning constitutional, when the garbage man began his early morning act with his clamorous ringing of the bell. Betsy had of late developed her own ideas about that door bell. She had developed the notion that anyone who rang that bell had hostile intentions. She felt that it was her duty to prevent any harm to the inhabitants of 'her' flat. Out for her morning constitutional, she heard the bell ring and she shook her head and bounded back to the flat at full speed. Rahul never had a chance to even hold her back as she wrenched her leash free from his hand.

The garbage man had piled the bags of garbage on his cart when Betsy barking furiously closed in. With remarkable agility he leapt up on his cart, on top of the heap. Betsy circled the cart slavering and growling and eyed him as if he was a particularly delectable morsel. She leapt at him, but he was just out of her reach and he cowered in terror before her. Just then Rahul came up and grabbed the leash and restrained her. She immediately became docile and let Rahul lead her away. The poor man was trembling when he came down, and promptly got a lecture on the consequences that befall persons who tease dogs, particularly Betsy. I don't know if the experience cured him of his desire to tease dogs because a couple of days later he left that job. He was replaced by an older man who was much kinder. Betsy barked at him too and one day he simply stood still while Betsy smelt him all over and gave a wag of her tail, as if to say, 'This one's all right'.

When Spring Was in the Air....

Betsy loved spring. The weather was just right, not too hot and not too cold. The nights were pleasant enough and there was so much to do and explore. Betsy loved that. A favourite word that she learnt as soon as it was said was 'walk!' That registered so well in her brain that soon she knew the timings for her walk and would run to get her leash, and bark impatiently at any delay. I was scared that if we were not swift enough the consequences may have been a dirty drawing room but Betsy quickly became house trained and my fears were proven unfounded. The combination of 'walk' and the fact that spring had come had made Betsy want to be in the nearby park for a large portion of her time. If the park was empty, as it often was, Betsy would be freed from her restraint and she would run as fast as she could, in sheer joy! Soon enough she would stop and enter the second phase - smelling. Her nose would be on the ground and she would be sniffing the ground, the bushes and anything that caught her fancy.

At times she would disappear behind a bush or behind a tree. At times I became alarmed and went in search but innocuously enough she had her nose exploring some mysteriously intriguing smell. A couple of times she was startled - once a stray dog burst out, chasing her. She prudently enough took shelter behind me and her head was visible as she peered at the intruder from behind me. She was very brave then! As she grew older these strategic retreats came to a halt. The reason was apparent. Most dogs were more scared of Betsy that Betsy of them. And our presence only strengthened her and empowered her to explore much more. Let's face it - Betsy was pure hunter and pure carnivore. She was soon stalking an unsuspecting squirrel when that poor creature had left the shelter and security of its tree. More often than not she managed to catch it and kill it. The same fate befell any sparrow or bird that was on the ground. Betsy would sink down and would be immobile; a short pause followed during which her prey was fooled into a reassuring complacency. A sharp dash, executed faultlessly before her victim could flee and the poor bird was in her jaws. Some she ate and some she discarded. But her tail would wag furiously at the end of these missions and she would expect a pat on her head for each creature she exterminated!

Betsy

AND THE

NEIGHBOURHOOD

Betsy was a bundle of joy and gave us her unconditional love, but that love did not extend to the neighbours or the garbage man. But in her own way she was compassionate and never bit a child though she frightened the daylights of most people! It sounds paradoxical but she was the most docile dog I have ever had. She just barked and snarled, a blood curling ferocious sound that would intimidate anyone nearby. That snarl was adequate and soon people began to avoid visiting us. She was extremely possessive about the house and it was a task she took very seriously. No one dared enter the house. The people in the neighbourhood were simply too petrified. Her powerful bark could be heard at the end of our block. The funny part was the neighbours at the end of the road knew that the garbage collector had come because of Betsy's bark. Betsy had a pathological hatred for the garbage man. Another person who she regarded as a low form of life on earth was the poor postman. Fortunately the advent of e-mails had more or less made him redundant but whenever he had to deliver a letter he would quickly drop the mail in the letter box and beat a hasty, dignified retreat, accompanied by barks and yelps as Betsy demanded that she be allowed to have a go at him.

Betsy
FOILS
A BURGLARY

Our car was parked outside our gate. We always ensured that it was locked and that was that as far as we were concerned. Betsy loved that car and had to be taken for a short drive every couple of days. Her head would stick out of the window as she sprawled across the entire back seat. Should any car come close Betsy would gnash her teeth and snarl at it. We would grab her collar but that was the extent of hostilities as far as she was concerned. Maybe she had included that car in her territorial domains, and regarded anyone coming near as having a sinister design on what she considered hers.

We were wakened at 2am by her furious barking. It was a different kind of barking and it seemed to have an undertone of urgency. I heard noises that seemed to originate from where we had parked our car. I switched on all the lights and that's when the alarm on the car began to hoot. Harry opened the front door and out charged Betsy. There was no one to be seen, but the car door had been opened. Harry closed the car door and reset the car alarm. Betsy ceased barking and began to sniff vigorously all around the car. Whoever it was had been disturbed and had run away. We went back indoors and reluctantly Betsy too came along. Clearly she was enjoying herself. We never ever faced a burglary or an attempt to break into the car again.

Watching TV

She enjoyed watching TV. She preferred songs to movies. There was one particularly catchy tune she relished - whenever she heard the song "Chaiya Chaiya" from the movie 'Dil Se' she would promptly sit facing the TV with her eyes and ears glued to the TV and would wag her tail till the song was over. She would then go back to whatever she was doing, even go back to sleep. It continued to be a favourite till it finally became stale enough to be taken off the air. She otherwise had no particular interest in TV.

Winter and The Other Seasons

A wag once remarked about the weather in North India that there are only two seasons - the hot season and the very hot season! Strictly it's not true but with the global warming we noticed that the winters had turned warmer and had become abbreviated into December and January. Betsy enjoyed the winters. Since I brushed her coat of fur every day I noticed that it would be particularly thick at that time of the year; she was very active at that time and would love to go to the park and play 'fetch the ball.' She played that with great enjoyment, excitedly chasing the ball, much to the dismay of others who were in the park. We would wait till when the park was empty and then let her loose in it. She had her own interpretation of what to do with the ball after she had grabbed it. She would refuse to part with it! This was invariably true if the ball belonged to some other children who were also playing in the park. Most inconsiderately, she would wait for her opportunity and would be off running furiously to grab the ball and triumphantly bring it back to us! She never ever attacked the children and soon enough they realised that in that big dog there lurked a child who was as playful as they were. When they played cricket the kids tried to enrol her as a fielder but Betsy regarded the ball as a trophy to bring home, rather than return it as part of the game. I guess she was not cut out for cricket, and we had to curtail her visit to the park if the children were at play. But it simply meant that Harry would take her for a long walk in the pleasant weather. She would run to get her leash, particularly if she felt it was her walk time and out the two of them would go. Harry is a solitary kind of a male and he enjoyed those walks with her. He once told me that they talked a lot during those times. It baffled me completely. Summer was the worst time of the year for Betsy; she could never take the harsh sun and the heat. She preferred being indoors in the cool of the air conditioning. The carpets that had been laid on the floor in winter were rolled and stowed in the loft. The cool floor was comforting and Betsy soon discovered some corners were the cool floor and a cool draft provided an antidote to the high temperature. Her bowl of water was always kept filled with clean and cool water. Her idea of a drink of water was to thrust almost her entire face into the water and lap it enthusiastically with her tongue; there was no gentleness of technique and the consequences were a puddle of water on the floor. This had to be mopped at regular intervals. She loved a glass of cold milk and this was consumed with such refinement of technique that not a drop fell on the ground. Summer was cruel to Betsy; her fur would shed and there would be tufts of the stuff that were adherent to the sofa, the bed, our clothes, on the crockery, in short, just about everywhere. I had to use a brush on her fur to remove the bits that were falling anyway; once she picked up an infection of the skin because of the heat and the vet clipped off most of her fur; shorn of her locks she looked really sheepish, but she recovered very fast and her coat grew back. Another antidote to the heat was to go to the lawn and dig a great big pit using her front paws, under the shade of a saal tree. She would then lie on the cool mud and sleep. This happened in Gurgaon where we moved there, but more about that later.

After the searing heat the arrival of the monsoon was as much an event as the visit of royalty, perhaps even more so. Betsy was only two months old when she encountered her first rain of the wet season. It had just started drizzling, I was really curious as to how she would respond to the rain because I just love the first shower of the season - the stale smells of the warm weather are replaced by the sweet smell of wet earth, and as by magic everything that is alive perks up. The birds chirp and suddenly there are hints of green replacing the burnt brown of the grass. It is bliss when the raindrops fall on one's face. I called Betsy to join me in the back yard when I realised that it was drizzling. She was perplexed and at the same time curious; her excitement became obvious as she sensed that I was enjoying myself in the rain, so she ventured to join me; when she felt the rain falling on her she began jumping around and yelping! It was an unforgettable sight. We both loved it. Once indoors I dried her with a towel and blow dried her fur. She had a bowl of warm milk and snoozed off. For Betsy getting drenched whenever opportunity presented was some kind of a canine nirvana. During every rainy season it was mandatory. We decided that we wanted to move to a less crowded locality and chose Gurgaon, in Haryana.

Betsy
AND THE
PEACOCKS

We moved to a ground floor unit in a house with a lawn in front and a yard behind, and facing a park. There was lots of open space all around because most of the plots on which houses would come up were still vacant and there was no major road in the vicinity. There was lots of space for a big golden retriever to run around and play. And yes as far as Betsy was concerned there was lots of small wildlife and things to hunt, and cats to chase. She loved the place! She would run, full of exuberance in the park, and then when a little out of breath would slow down. All the while she would look back, as to enquire, 'What? Aren't you coming?' Her tail would wag ferociously and I would imagine that if that was the flapping wing of a bird, Betsy might become airborne!

We were pretty delighted too with being in Gurgaon as after living in a cramped region like Vasant Kunj, Gurgaon was like a breath of fresh air for all of us. We had moved into our new place, and the day went past in a blur of unpacking and arranging our bits and pieces of furniture; we had to look after the children and look after Betsy who sniffed every corner in delight. Exhausted we stumbled into bed. Promptly at the crack of dawn we were awaked by the cry of a peacock. It seemed to originate close by. I peeped through the window, and saw a wild peacock, accompanied by his harem of three peahens sauntering outside our gate. They were pecking for food and every now and then, the peacock would ruffle his long graceful tail of feathers. A shrill cry would escape his beak and the peahens would respectfully acknowledge it by uttering shorter squawks. The entourage leisurely passed by our house. The sight was undoubtedly enthralling for a person, city born and bred. In Delhi there are no peacocks. The noise that the birds made had woken up the house. Harry and the kids got up and rushed outside to see the peacocks taking their morning constitutional. They gaped as it was a sight that city dwellers never see, but is commonplace in villages or where the population is less. Peacocks are adaptive birds, but only in a semi wild environment.

Betsy too had charged out with the rest of the family. She had never encountered a bird that was the size of a peacock and she barked loudly at them; she rushed towards them, but the closed gate of our house put a stop to that charge. The peacock brigade was unfazed by her noise. They simply ignored her; some avian sense must have told them that the barred gate prevented a slavering, crazed canine from hurtling at them, intent on their destruction.

The novelty soon wore off because the peacocks visited every day, but their timings became variable. They preferred to stroll past in the cooler early hours of summer and somewhat later when winter had set in. But to Betsy they posed a formidable challenge. She hated them, and as the area outside of our gate represented a sphere of influence that was hers to dominate, it was inconceivable that a few birds could simply stroll past unchallenged. And the only obstacle to their decimation by Betsy was the gate, which we took great pains to lock every single night before retiring.

Once Betsy did encounter a peacock and charged madly towards it. To any observer her intentions were homicidal; the peacock thought so too as Betsy rushed towards him, barking ferociously. He smartly flew and perched on the branches of a nearby tree well out of her reach, and gave her a look of utter contempt. Clearly Betsy did not anticipate that the peacock would so uncharitably fly out of her reach and taken aback she noisily barked at him from the base of the tree. A minute or so later, and offended by this noise, the peacock flew to the roof of an adjacent building in haughty disdain. Betsy taken aback could only watch it go. She became quiet and meekly followed me home. She noisily slurped water from her bowl as I am sure that all that barking was thirsty work, and settled down and went off to sleep in a cool corner.

Betsy

ENCOUNTERS

A BUFFALO

Time flew and Betsy was being taken in the car to the vet for her for her booster shots. She was in her favourite seat - the rear seat by the window. The glass window was down and she was happily enjoying the rush of air as we cruised sedately. That is when Betsy spotted a buffalo. In Gurgaon, Haryana, it is customary for villagers to keep cows and buffaloes. These creatures are turned loose after milking and they roam the streets looking for food. Towards the evening these milch animals are sufficiently smart to find their way back home.

The buffalo is a calm unemotional kind of animal and my guess is that it would take a lot of effort to get that creature exited. She was happily chomping on a crop of luxuriant grass that had sprouted on a vacant plot, oblivious to her surroundings, lost in a digestive nirvana. That is, till Betsy spotted her. I think a kind of rage came over Betsy at the sight of that large beast chewing away. Betsy jumped out of the window, from the moving car and charged towards the buffalo; surprised, Harry slowed down and fortunately the road was completely deserted. Betsy barked at the buffalo forcing the startled animal to retreat; Betsy quite satisfied with that, realised that she would be left behind, ran towards the car and jumped back in through the same window. It all happened so fast that we were taken by surprise. We became extraordinarily careful after that and made sure she was secured with her collar even we were ever going out.

A Lawn Becomes An Impossible Dream.

Betsy use to go bananas when we would water the lawn. She had to get wet. Invariably she had to be hosed with water and she would feel such relief that she would flop down in a puddle and roll over it. In the process she would become muddy and had to be hosed all over again. If she found that the lawn was already watered, she would splash in the puddles and roll in the wet grass making happy noises; she would then proceed to dig a pit and snooze off in it. A well groomed lawn and Betsy were not compatible. A big muddy pit was. And no flowers please, thank you very much. Both jasmine and marigolds are tropical flowers that are easy to grow and that give predictable results should one go to the effort of planting them; so said the article in the magazine on garden decor. What the author of that article had not reckoned with was the presence of a great big, slavering golden retriever whose idea of a good time was to either dig up the entire plant or to delicately bite off each jasmine flower and eat it. The kids once put the marigold flower garland around Betsy's neck. She was overjoyed and refused to have it removed! She slept with it around her neck and it could only be taken off the next day. We soon abandoned our ideas of a lawn bounded with bushes on which pretty flowers would bloom; if we wanted Betsy we had to settle for a muddy pit instead.

Betsy

AND

THE COUCH

If there is one thing that the husband loves it is a peaceful read of the daily newspaper, with a cup of tea. So immersed does the man gets in reading his paper that normal conversation is impossible. The only times his eyes leave the newspaper is to seek out his cup of tea. A sip later, the husband is riveted to the daily news once again. A bomb could explode next to him and I bet he would not be disturbed. To make matters worse he subscribes to three newspapers and what really gets him irritated is if the newspaper delivery boy delays the arrival of these chronicles. Husbands are a strange breed - the news is never nice; it is a daily quota of crime, crooked people, hatred and war that is served in differing proportions daily - but it has to be consumed rigorously, in silence, and daily, ignoring everything that occurs all around while its digestion is in process.

In our house news is accessed like it would be in the office of the news editor of a global newspaper. There have been times when the radio had been giving its version, and the TV has been showing live news and the newspaper is being scanned, all at the same time. Harry swears that he can listen to both the TV and the radio at the same time; I am not too sure if he can read the news at the same time as well. What I do know is that he can fall asleep doing all three. If the radio were to be switched off he will wake up promptly and complain that the noise being made all around is too much and disturbs him!

To ensure that the sanctity of this daily ritual of newspaper worship is maintained, Harry went and got himself a couch. It took him a month to locate what he wanted. It was made by a craftsman in a nearby village and was a traditional couch, crafted out of woven rope, put together in an intricate weave. It was a beautiful piece, common in villages of yore, but today replaced by the ubiquitous plastic chair. This was placed in an open area near the lawn/muddy pit; a potted palm was lovingly purchased and placed next to the couch. A low table was rustled up so that the newspapers and the cup of tea could be in handy reach and I suspect so arranged that the cup could be grasped without having to remove the eyes from the newspaper. It was the perfect arrangement, like the Japanese have the art of origami, Harry had perfected the art of what I call, 'The worship of the morning news.'

He did not know it then, but as the saying goes, there is many a slip between the proverbial cup and the lip. That slip was provided by Betsy. When Betsy saw the couch and the potted palm so lovingly placed close to it, she was convinced that this arrangement was placed for her benefit. She promptly and easily leapt up onto the couch and sprawled on it. She made herself fairly comfortable and fell asleep on it. When she woke up she realised that the fronds of the palm tree were in easy reach. She set upon them with gusto and ripped them off the plant, giving it a threadbare look on one side. The other side being less accessible was so far spared.

When Harry saw the fate of his couch and his palm he was quite reasonably furious. One of the things about Betsy was her ability to understand the moods of the human beings around her, and I guess she could understand that chewing up a potted plant may not go down too well with them. What she could not comprehend was that the ownership of the couch was not hers. She was convinced that we had purchased the couch for her to sprawl, or to rub her body against it; whenever opportunity presented itself, she would leap up on it and relax. One day when we were not at home, Betsy decided that the spared fronds of the palm needed her attention as well; she attacked them and left the palm devoid of any branch whatsoever. The trunk of the plant remained intact, as a poignant remembrance of its former glory, and of the dream of my husband. We shifted the plant to a corner in our garden, but I think the treatment it had endured was simply too much for it and it dried up and withered away.

What was the fate of the couch? Betsy refused to relinquish her right to occupy it and for a while it was a tussle between her and Harry. He would yell at her and she would jump off it with a hurt look on her face. The moment his back was turned she would promptly reoccupy it. It became a little tatty and rights to it were relinquished by Harry in her favour. It could not take her jumping on and jumping off and began to fall apart and finally had to be discarded.

Illness and Surgery

I ensured that Betsy received her injections for distemper, rabies and other doggie diseases well within the prescribed time. We were fortunate to find Dr Inder, a kind hearted and competent vet who loved his feline and canine charges as much as they loved him. All of us are indebted to him for the expert care he rendered whenever Betsy took ill. Overall she was a healthy animal, and we took great care with her diet and exercise. I personally groomed her and her coat glowed. As any good looking woman gets her share of admirers, Betsy too had a regular fan club who followed her. All this incidentally was before the age of facebook and twitter.

Betsy was out playing withe a ball in the park. I would throw it and she would run after it, and usually grab it while it was still moving. She normally brought it back and dropped it nearby so that it could be thrown again for her to retreive. This game could be played endlessly and Betsy never tired of it. This time I noted that she did not seem as energetic as she normally was. I did not give it much attention but I cut short the game and we headed home soon after. Betsy ran on ahead. That night she did not eat or drink anything. She preferred to sit quietly and I thought that she might be simply tired and I let her be. The children needed my help with their homework and the house chores needed to be done. I mentioned to Harry that Betsy might be unwell, but Harry was immersed in his work and grunted. I took it that it meant that all was well. For a wife several years into marriage and a couple of children later, the science of interpretation of grunts made by the male spouse is ridiculously easy and accurate. Nobody that I know can interpret grunts made by Harry with the ease that I can. We were awakened that night with the sound of Betsy moaning in pain. It was so very distressing and after switching on the lights both of us looked at Betsy with concern. She lay on her side and would not move. I sat next to her on the floor and stroked her head; she wagged her tail feebly. Her eyes looked sunken and had lost their sparkle. I knew we had an emergency on our hands. It was four in the morning, and I knew that there are no available services for dogs at that hour. We were on our own, till we could get her to a vet. Betsy groaned again in pain and it was a heart wrenching sound. I looked at Harry. He was efficiently assembling a pain killing injection which he proceeded to inject into her. A few minutes late she was calmer and apparently the pain appeared to have reduced. An hour or so later the pain seemed to have recurred as she began to moan again. Harry reached for the phone and a short while later I was on my way, with Betsy lying on the car seat beside me, to see Dr. Inder. Harry could not come, as he had a full OPD to manage. I promised him I would keep him posted.

Dr. Inder carefully examined Betsy; she was in a great deal of pain and there was a discharge from her vaginal passage. His face grave Dr. Inder looked shrewdly at me. In a level voice he explained that Betsy had developed pus in her uterus and this would need to be removed. He added that he was willing to try antibiotics first and surgery could be a second option. To me it sounded as if he was offering me a way out in case I did not choose an operation. I grasped what was on his mind. I am not a doctor but my father was a busy GP, and two of my brothers are busy doctors, and my husband is a busy surgeon. Our house was always full of doctors who spoke only 'shop' at home and a lot of medical wisdom had rubbed off on me. I was perfectly aware that there are many would not spend money on treating a sick animal, who may perish despite treatment.

On the humane side Betsy needed an operation and delay in trying out medical remedies for what clearly was a surgical problem was to my mind quite illogical. It was my call. I told him to go ahead and operate. A consent form was produced for me to sign. It stated that I would not hold Dr. Inder responsible if my dog died during or after the surgery. I signed. 'Just hurry up', I said.

She was taken up for surgery a short while later. He removed her uterus; later he told me that I had brought Betsy to him in the very nick of time, and for a while it seemed that it would be touch and go. He good health, Dr. Inder's surgical skills, and modern antibiotics pulled her through. She was very close to being herself in 48 hours.

The wound healed perfectly. A week later she was playing in the park again. Betsy came under the knife a second time for a lump she developed in one of her teats. It was a painless lump and I discovered it when brushing her. I was worried when it began to grow, and I reported it to Harry, who promptly took her to Dr. Inder. Harry is a spine surgeon. He is super efficient if he encounters any illness and I was glad he was around to take these decisions. Betsy was active, running around, barking, eating well and apparently healthy. Yet there was this lump that was slowly and painlessly increasing in size. Dr. Inder too was concerned and we discussed the possibility of a cancerous growth; he advised an excision of the growth and its biopsy. Harry promptly said yes and though I had reservations about operations, I too fell in line. Surgery was scheduled at his clinic a day or so later and I took Betsy home with trepidation in my heart. She was taken to the clinic where Dr. inder performs his operations on the following day. She had been deprived of food and water for several hours prior to her surgery and was a bit puzzled about it. When it was time to leave for her surgery, she realised a car ride was in the offing and cheerfully leapt into the car and took her coveted position by the window which was rolled down to let her enjoy the rush of air on her face. Harry was with me and both of us were silent. I stroked her head and she gaily wagged her tail. She did something unusual for her - she put her head on my lap instead of sticking it out of the window as was her wont, and let me stroke her. She sighed and a few minutes later she was her normal self. Was she comforting me or was I comforting her?

At clinic she was her normal self and took great pleasure in barking at some of the other canine patients that were visiting the good doctor. She was taken up for surgery and Dr. Inder excised one of her mammary glands completely. It went well, and the wound healed perfectly. She had a host of medicines to take which she did with remarkable cheerfulness. Her recovery was completely uneventful.

Betsy was friendly with Dr. Inder and I would say much less kindly disposed towards his assistants; she greeted Dr. Inder with her tail wagging in joyful abandon, as she was greeting a long lost soul. She greeted his assistants with a snarl and quick snap of her jaws if one of their digits was in her reach. She regarded them as her mortal enemies. She had an excellent memory and once someone was in her bad books he or she was destined to remain there. This meant being snarled at and snapped at and perhaps losing a piece of anatomy if not sufficiently careful. Along with garbage collectors, postmen, cyclists, children, milkman, delivery boy, cats, rats, peacocks, all birds, pigs, buffaloes and cows, Dr. Inder's assistants were assigned a low place in her order of things.

Betsy was destined to have yet another encounter with Dr. Inder and his assistants. She injured her hind paw on the right side and sustained a fracture and a wound in one part of it. When it did not heal despite dressings and medication, Dr. Inder operated. It was debrided, and a part of the diseased bone removed. It healed after that.

Betsy

AND

KITTY

Like most dogs Betsy would go berserk if she ever saw, smelt or heard a cat mew. She had encountered cats in her prowl around the house, and she knew that they were really delightful to chase. She had never been able to catch one though, possibly because the feline was smart enough to shin up the nearest ledge or tree and at times at a height just about adequate to keep her out of reach. Betsy would go berserk; there would be loud and excited yelps, angry barks, and the sound of Betsy panting as she valiantly tried to jump and grab a mouthful of cat. But though she had never ever caught one, she harboured an unsparing pathological hatred of that species.

It so happened that one cold wintery day we had gone to shop for groceries. It was pretty late in the evening and when we were about to sit in the car when I heard a mewing sound near the car door. I glanced all around and there she was - a tiny frail little kitten who looked at me straight in the eye and gave a mew, almost like a sob. We searched for the mother who was not to be seen anywhere; the mewing was so pathetic and helpless that we felt obliged to take the poor creature home. We named her Kitty. I poured some warm milk into a bowl and soaked a slice of bread in it. She lapped it up and I made a bed from an old bed sheet and tucked her in. Betsy was extremely disturbed as the smell of the newcomer was that of a species clearly hostile; not surprisingly she took an instant dislike to the intruder. We kept Kitty in the upstairs room with my daughter, away from Betsy. The latter was aware that the intruder was hidden somewhere and she made every attempt to locate her. There was a pleading look in her eyes and a strong hint of malice in her demeanour. I knew that she felt that we were cheating her out of one of the big pleasures of canine life, that of chasing a cat, but we were unrelenting. Kitty was with us for a month and

Betsy made no attempts to be her friend. She grew into a beauty and we found a home for her. We never forgot her and neither did Betsy. Years later whenever the word 'kitty' was mentioned Betsy would go bonkers; she would run around the house looking for that feline. We realised that as long as Betsy was around, a cat as a pet was impossible. We did not know it then, but we were going to get a pug as a pet...

Michelle Wong

My daughter, Aditi had gone to Jaipur to visit her friend at their farm house; their pug had littered seven pups. All had died except one whose tenacious hold on life was weakening. Aditi looked at the solitary pup, and the callous attitude of the owners towards their dogs was unbearable. She could not fathom the fact that had the pups been looked after they would probably have survived. She could not bear that if she did nothing, the solitary survivor faced certain death. She called me and related the story. Then she simply said about the last of the litter, "Ma if I don't bring her home she too will surely die." I understood that behind these deaths was a story of neglect, pure and simple; vets are scarce especially in isolated communities. I heard myself say, "Get her over and let's see what we can do". Aditi put her in a car, wrapped her in a sheet and drove back. When I looked at what Aditi had brought I was too amazed for words. The pup was as big as my palm and looked more like a rat. She was ten days old having been born on 3rd April 2008. My daughter arrived late in the evening and I hadn't the foggiest as to how she should be fed. In my teens I had rescued a number of baby squirrels who had fallen out of their nesting places in trees, and I had fed them with rubber dropper (not the plastic dropper). So I did the same. We bought baby milk powder and made a cup of milk feed. The pup was famished - she gulped the warm milk as soon as the dropper came into contact with her mouth. Slowly I fed her drop by drop and soon she fell asleep. I swaddled her in one of my old shirts to keep her warm and we placed the little one in a pink plastic basket that had a lid. I did not want big Betsy to attack her. We lined one side of her basket with newspaper and padded the other half with a soft cloth; a towel was draped on three sides of the basket to keep away any draught. I made a chart to keep a record of the number of feeds and the time. I decided that I would feed her every two hours. She needed a name and she needed to be seen by Dr Inder. After much debate between the kids as to what to name the pug, we zeroed in on a name; we decided to name her Michelle Wong, or simply Miss Wong as pugs as a breed are from China.

Dr. Inder

On the following day Aditi and I took Michelle Wong to Dr. Inder. She weighed 668 grams and was just about 4" in length. He was amazed that she was actually alive. He gravely said that she was a premature pup and needed careful care and lots of love. His face was grim, and I felt that he left unsaid the bit about her survival; I felt that she had hung on all these days and she would survive. He put her on an IV drip and we watched her lying there as the fluid went into her. We took her to his clinic every alternate day, where he pushed in intravenously nutritional supplements and vitamins. This went on for a month. There was progress at home too; from feeding her with a dropper we began feeding her with a milk bottle, gradually increasing the amount of baby feed. I encountered a problem. Michelle began to throw up and a few minutes after the bottle she would bring out the entire feed. Her tummy which had become convex after the feed would become concave again. I began to worry and it got me thinking - I actually began burping her just like I did for my own babies and it worked! After her feed I would hold her upright and stroke her back till she burped. Michelle stopped vomiting. Gradually she began to gain weight;

she could not tolerate fresh milk, but relished powdered milk and we stuck with that. When she was six months old I began weaning her off the milk powder and gradually added solid feeds. Her first solid feed was natural yoghurt and she loved it. In a phased way we included in her diet, clear stew with vegetables, and bits of boneless chicken. I added oats after a few weeks and a little later fruits like papaya and bananas. These remain her favourites till today.

She began to take wobbly steps. I did not have a play pen or an enclosed area which would curtail her movements, so gradually our bed became her territorial zone; we would place a waterproof covering and place a bedspread over it. It sufficed to let her roam around on it and yet it kept her safe. To prevent her from falling off I piled sheets and quilts all around the edges of the bed, almost converting it into a fort. I was worried that Betsy would somehow get into the room with unpredictable results.

Betsy did not know Michelle was home

Betsy was a puzzled dog. There was something going on, so secretive and she did not know exactly what that was. She was of course aware that there was a stranger in the house, possibly another dog. I was worried that if Betsy encountered her she may attack her or severely bite her. Betsy was a hunter and we knew that she had trapped, killed and devoured birds, squirrels, rats and God alone knew what else. I decided that I would gradually introduce the two.

When Michelle was few months old I gave her a sheet on which Betsy slept and similarly Betsy received a sheet on which Michelle had slept. The effect on Betsy was simply electrifying. She sat on the ground next to the sheet and spent at least ten minutes smelling it. It was a thorough olfactory examination. I could almost feel the impact that registered in her mind, 'Hey! There's another dog living in this house besides me'. Michelle may have had a similar feeling.

One morning after Michelle had been fed, and lodged safely in the security of her fort, I allowed Betsy into the room. She was full of curiosity and sniffed all around and wagged her tail as if to say, 'Hey! Let's be friends!' She was consumed with curiosity and wanted to leap into Michelle's secure zone. Michelle took one look at Betsy and dived for shelter under the quilts. I was pleased that there was no antagonism or aggression displayed by Betsy towards Michelle and I felt that the two would get along very well. However I wasn't taking chances and was always around at these introductory meetings so that hostilities did not break out. When Michelle was the size of a two month golden retriever and yes, much bigger than a rat I put her on the ground for the two to sniff and smell each other. I think that somewhere in my mind there existed the picture of Betsy chom- ping down a rat with gusto and I didn't want that to happen to poor Michelle. I imagine that Betsy was secretly amused by Michelle's size or was it that she aro- used the maternal and motherly instincts? Betsy never ever barked at Michelle or tried to attack her. They became the best of friends and had many adventures together.

Betsy BECOMES A MENTOR

Michelle would simply not bark. Betsy would bark at the slightest noise, or the tiniest disturbance. A short and aggressive growl, full of latent menace was enough to deter all but the foolhardy. Michelle was full of play and would climb all over Betsy, smelling her, biting her. A particularly favourite part that seemed succulent to Michelle was Betsy's tail. Betsy never retaliated and if offended would simply get up and walk away, apparently affronted. Michelle would watch, a little puzzled, and then run after her as if to say, 'Hey! I never meant any offence!' I noted that Michelle a tiny pug would try to copy Betsy at times. When Betsy barked, Michelle would also tried to bark; the sound that came from the former was like an explosion going off at close quarters, and hardly any sound emanated from the latter. In fact Michelle was always silent and would not bark. When she did, no sound would come. I began to call these 'silent barks'. We tried to get Michelle to bark by telling her, 'Woof! Woof! Michelle,' and all it did was to get her to run around in a confused way. Betsy having heard, 'Woof!' would let forth a volley of barks, more like noisy firecrackers blasting away. It was then that Michelle would loosen up and let fly a yelp or two and a series of silent barks. Harry, Rahul and Aditi would burst into paroxysms of laughter. I would be concerned about the silent barks. Who has ever seen a dog bark with no noise issuing forth? It seemed so anti canine of her; it was like a cannon firing but with no noise. I decided that I would speak to Dr. Inder about it.

Betsy was a mentor to Michelle. Michelle learnt to bark when she heard the door bell and guard the house like Betsy does. They spent time playing, sleeping and eating meals and sharing a bone. They would even watch TV together. It was delightful to see them so compatible with one another, irrespective of their ages and breed.

Michelle would climb over Betsy, and then tumble over to the other side. She would chew her ears and smell them. Betsy simply and good naturedly tolerated these. Now and then she too would smell Michelle. The latter would simply freeze till the smelling session was over.

Betsy RESCUES MICHELLE

Michelle never barked or growled even when she was two year old. She continued to make soft grunting noises which one could barely hear. I had spoken to Dr. Inder and he said that her vocal chords were weak and there was nothing that one could do about that. The volume of her bark would increase over time. So I had ceased to worry about her barking and when she became older her barking became loud and clear. But I am going ahead of my story. When I had visitors at home I would generally put both the dogs in my bedroom so they were never alarmed or troubled. After the departure of our guests, the dogs were let loose again. This standard operating procedure was adhered to whenever we had visitors. With the departure of our guests the bedroom doors were opened.

Once after our guests had left, and the door of the bedroom was opened, Betsy bounded out, went and settled on her rug while I got busy with the clearing up. It was only after an hour did I realize that Michelle was missing. I called her name, and not seeing her, I searched the house. No sign of her. I went to the front yard and the backyard all looked in all her favourite places; Michelle was nowhere to be seen. I was shattered. I flopped on the sofa stunned, wondering where Michelle was. All sorts of ideas flashed in my head. Betsy had noted that I was disturbed. Her ears were cocked and her intelligent eyes held a question, 'What's up?' I told Betsy to go and look for Michelle. 'Go find Michelle', I told her. She wagged her tail, and she began sniffing around in the drawing room. She kept sniffing near the cupboard and started wagging her tail as if she found something. Watching her suddenly get all excited, it struck me that I had not looked behind the cupboard. Sure enough Michelle was sitting there, all curled up. Somehow she had squeezed herself in the gap between the two cupboards, and could not come out. I pushed one of the cupboards forward and managed to squeeze in from behind the cupboard, and rescue her. She was cold and frightened. What an ordeal for her! I gave her a cuddle and Betsy was so happy she noisily slurped Michelle all over her face.

The kids were simply appalled when they heard what had transpired, and it was Rahul who came up with the idea that we should tie a little bell to her collar. We did precisely that and wherever Michelle went we knew she was fine by the tinkling sound it made. We continued to fit a bell to her collar till she was four years old.

On another occasion, Michelle managed to clamber up a few steps that led to a bedroom on the first floor. She could not climb down and slept off on one of the steps. I went half crazy looking for her. Again this was before any kind of electronic collar was invented - the ones that emit a bleep or flash a light to indicate their location when a button on a remote control is pressed. But I had Betsy to help and all I had to do was to tell Betsy,' Go find Michelle', and she did precisely that. She barked loudly when she had located her.

Best Buddies

Betsy and Michelle played every morning after breakfast. Michelle's favourite game was chasing Betsy's long bushy tail. Betsy would raise her tail and Michelle would jump to catch it or Betsy would go round in circles and Michelle would go round chasing her tail. Michelle would wait till Betsy was asleep; she would then pounce on Betsy's tail and wake her up. If Betsy was offended, she would get up and walk away, but this was rare. Usually she was happy to play.

Since Michelle had a small mouth we got her some discarded soft toys. Betsy loved them, and would try to whisk them away for herself. Michelle kept a proprietarily eye on them and at times it would come down to a tug of war, each holding a part of the soft toy. Michelle usually lost, or the toy came apart.

Another favourite was to simply chase a ball around in the back yard. Betsy would have the ball and trot around while Michelle would excitedly chase her. She could never get the better of Betsy. After a good game they would cuddle up and sleep. Michelle always slept very close to her, almost touching her. I guess she derived comfort from that.

Mealtimes

Michelle had become quite the charmer by the time she turned two. Whenever we had visitors, Michelle would come to greet them. Being small and delicate she touched a chord of maternal feelings in our female visitors and much fussing and stroking was carried out. She lapped up all the affection that was showered upon her. She learnt to have her own way and took it for granted that visitors to the Bajaj house were dog lovers and were or were going to become her fans. Most did become her fans and she can open her own fan club. Some of Harry's colleagues and their children were so enamoured that they began to ask for her to be mated so they could claim a pup. When I patiently told them about the work involved in rearing a dog, house training her, grooming, feeding the enthusiasm began to wane somewhat. Most of these chats were over dinner with both Betsy and Michelle eating with the family from their own separate bowls. Both were fiercely adamant about this and since the entire family would have a meal perhaps it was only natural that the two would also share a meal with us. In any case food for both the dogs was served together.

The behaviour of both Betsy and of Michelle at mealtimes was unique. Betsy would wait patiently for her meal to be served. She never fussed even it was slightly late and would wag her tail and devour every morsel, licking her plate absolutely clean. Betsy was always remarkably well behaved. Michelle, when hungry would bark an irritable sharp bark of protest, particularly if she was served lower in the pecking order. After breakfast was served, Michelle would always inspect Betsy's bowl first, leaving hers behind. She would sniff the food and Betsy recognising her immaturity and impatience would simply allow her. She would only then attack the food in her own bowl. Betsy was always the well behaved dog.

The amusing bit was Michelle invariably left food in her bowl; distracted she would wander off and I imagine she always thought that it would be waiting for her whenever she felt she wanted to eat something. Crafty Betsy was one who would never let an opportunity like this to go by. Very slowly and carefully she would begin an imperceptible crawl towards the food in Michelle's bowl, and having reached there undetected as she imagined, she would rapidly polish off every morsel in that bowl as well. Rahul was impressed with her ability to lick the bowl clean and named her as the vacuum cleaner! She would demolish anything and everything that came her way. It was in this manner that Betsy came to enjoy fruits. Michelle had developed a love for papaya while Betsy didn't much care for it. Since Michelle's bowl invariably had papaya, and Betsy would never leave it behind, I recognised that like Michelle, Betsy too started enjoying papaya. Michelle loves bananas and soon Betsy too began eating them. They both loved mangoes and were given this as a treat at times!

Betsy had turned 14. We had noted that she had slowed down and though she still loved to catch the odd bird, she was increasingly content to let things be. She preferred to lie in the sun, something she never did in her younger days. She would frequently limp, and Dr. Inder said that she had developed arthritis of her hips. Harry would joke that she needed a hip replacement, an operation done for the diseased hip in adult human beings. I would look at her with concern and would give her calcium and the medicines that the vet had prescribed; often I had to force her to swallow these and she would do so reluctantly. Her front teeth had fallen off and when she ever so infrequently snarled, we would see her toothless gums!

In June, she deteriorated and we noted that she had difficulty in using her hind legs. Visits to Dr. Inderbecame weekly and then daily. Drips and injections were routine, and the Doctor would attend lovingly and immediately, rather than letting her wait in a long line of his mostly canine patients. His staff too had noted the change. Betsy used to snarl at them in her younger days, but she rarely did now....

One day we noted that she could not move. Her hind legs could not support her and she could not even stand. We carried her outside to do her business, but she could not and only soiled herself. She was in pain, and her eyes had a distant look. I knew that we had run out of options.

It was the 5th of August; we carried her into our car and made her comfortable and took her to Dr. Inder for the last time. The house was silent. Our man Friday, Hari Om, could not bear it and broke down. He bawled like a baby. Harry comforted him. Michelle was subdued and sensed that her friend was seriously unwell. In her own way she knew the inevitable.

Dr. Inder examined Betsy and explained that she was paralyzed from the waist down and the chances of her recovery were negligible; we would reduce her suffering a great deal if we put her down. I wanted to take her back and nurse her, but I realized that it was only going to prolong her misery. I wanted to remember her as she was, running excitedly in the park, chasing squirrels and hunting birds and not as a paralyzed dog soiling herself. Everybody was looking at me and I nodded my head in agreement. I stroked her head for the last time. Tears flew freely from the eyes of all four of us and even the staff of Dr. Inder, normally ebullient were quiet.

Dr. Inder administered a double dose of an anaesthetic agent and Betsy became silent forever. We wrapped her in her sheet, and took her body to the electric crematorium and cremated her. The next day we collected her ashes in a mud pot and brought them home. A day later we drove to Garh, where the most sacred Ganges flows and in a quiet bend of that mighty river, each of us said a silent prayer and let her ashes mingle withher running waters.

Life after Betsy
Michelle today

Michelle's surrogated mother was no more, but Michelle looked for her everywhere. We removed her feeding bowl and her bed. Michelle was quiet and refused to eat. No amount of coaxing would get her to swallow even a mouthful. She developed a fever and once again it was Dr. Inder who saw her through with medication and intravenous drips. Finally she started to eat and we all heaved a collective sigh of relief. Today Michelle is her normal self, demanding to be fed and cuddled. She has not forgotten Betsy and if in our conversation she hears that name her ears stand up and her eyes and demeanour become alert. I maintain a disciplined protocol with her, and though one may be accused of 'humanising' one's dogs, one is always grateful for the joy they brought to one's life.

Postscript

Both Betsy and Michelle taught us to be kind to all animals; they too have emotions and feelings. It is just that they express these differently and it takes an astute person to comprehend what is left unsaid or is expressed in a different way. There is an expression called, 'It's a dog's life.' To understand this one only needs to see a cowering street canine on the night of Deepavaliwhen crackers are bursting all around and the poor creatures can only cower in drains, in bushes or any place where they find sanctuary. I am utterly revolted by the stories of dogs having crackers tied to their tails, or similar insane acts of cruelty inflicted on them as a means of spectator entertainment. Why is it that we see dogs roaming on the streets in the cities of India and not in the cities of Europe, America or Australia? These are developed countries which have overcome the problem of street garbage and slums.

The problem of stray dogs will stay in our cities as long as these dogs have access to garbage and as long as there are slums and slum dwellers. Garbage is a source of food to strays, and what we term as garbage may be appetising to them! Slum and street dwellers keep dogs as free roaming pets. In the developed world both these are non issues and the problem of strays is resolved. In our cities both of these are going to be around and the only way to overcome these is to neuter strays, or have people adopt strays. Feeding strays with leftovers does not contribute to the problem and is an act of kindness. Of course it goes without stating the obvious that feeding strays should not cause a nuisance to the public, and should be done responsibly. I would urge people to be kind to these creatures who are also created by the same God.

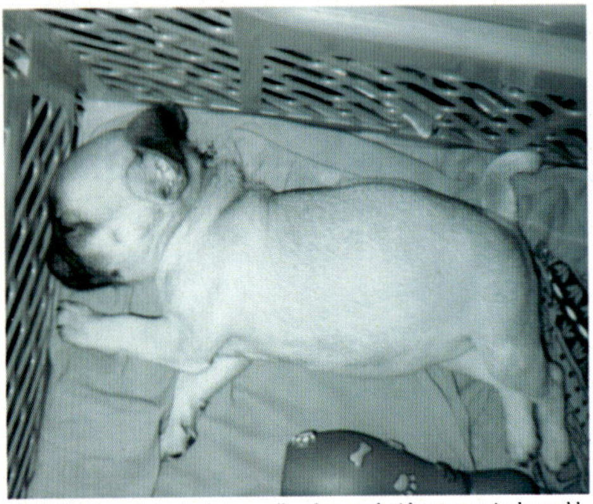

Michelle, secure in her basket, soundly asleep, and without a care in the world

"What a Long Day, My Neck is Really Sore. Got Surgery Done."

"Drool Drool!... Hurry Up Ma I Can't Stay Put any Longer."

Betsy AND Michelle

"Michelle!..... look!..... fish!"

"Come on Ma!..... We Are Hungry!.... We can Smell Something Yummy!"

Come on Betsy Jump!

lle made her entry into our lives a few days after her birth

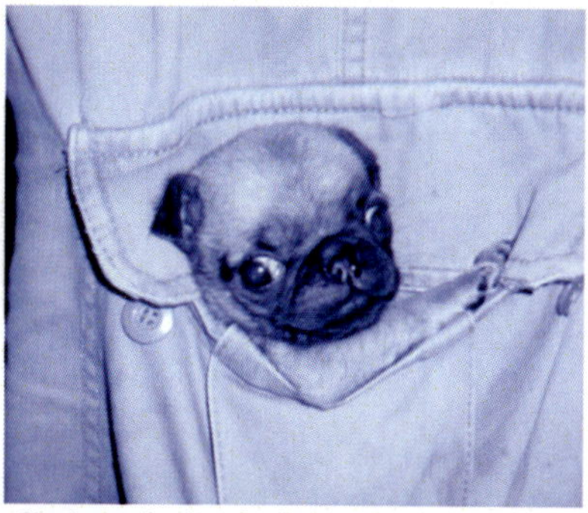

She always enjoyed travel and sight seeing in comfort and style

Quallity time with Papa!

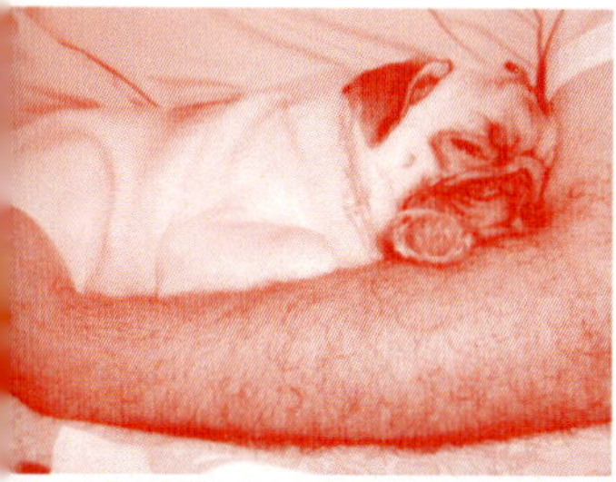

Some of Michelle's Favourite Sleeping Places!

Nosey, Nosey!

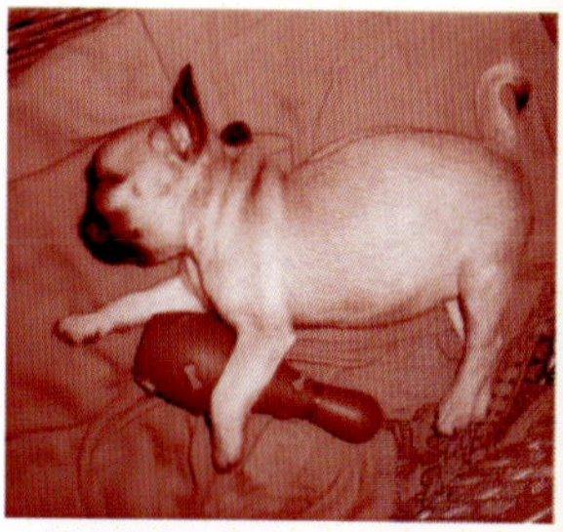

Michelle Soundly Asleep In Her Basket
Without A Care In The World

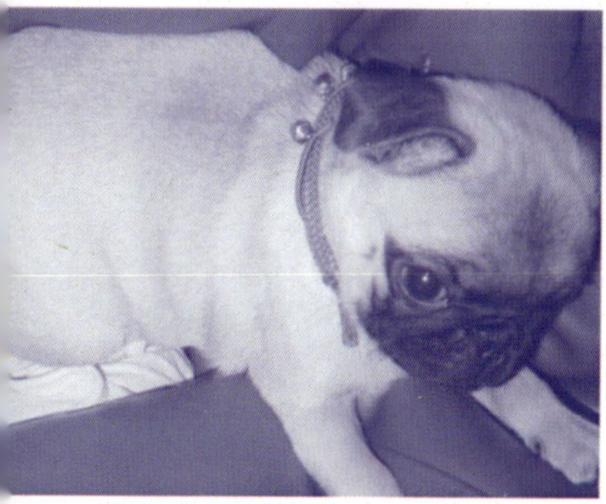

"Hey! get me out of here, somebody...."

"Some body please tell me what do
I do with this..... it smells nice though!"

"Oh Boy! My favourite place for a Snooze!"

That's My Buddy Rahul

"I am not keeping too well.
visit to the vet. is such an ordeal for me."

Peek a Boo!

"Back off guys I ain't in the Mood"

"First Solid Meal..." Great Stuff This!

"Seriously!... you dont want to play?... ho

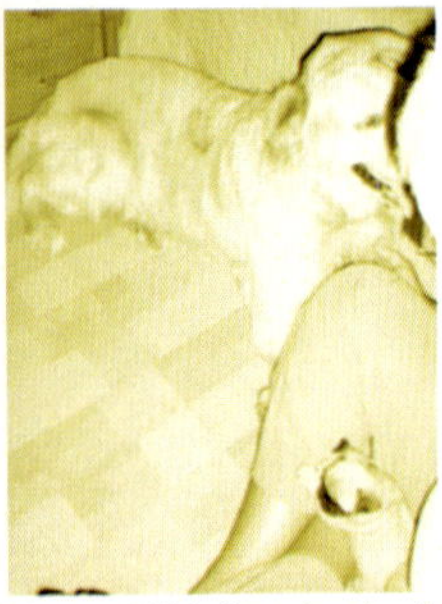

Betsy and Michelle are introduced to each other

"All right Michelle, if you say so, lets go and play!"

"Come on Ma!... We are hungry!... We can smell something yummy!"

"This sure beats sitting on the flo Sorry, but I ain't moving!"

What a Treat!

"Hmmm... Hey Mishu! Did You Have A Bath?"

Back from work need to Hug My Buddy.

Love is Sharing Ma's Bed

"I'm bored! now where is everyone?"

"Wake up Lazy Bones! Let's go Play!"

Betsy and Michelle

Betsy AND Michelle